A CRACK IN THE WALL

BY MARY ELIZABETH HAGGERTY

ILLUSTRATED BY RUBÉN DE ANDA

Lee & Low Books Inc. • New York

LEE & LOW BOOKS Inc., 228 East 45th Street, New York, NY 10017

Printed in Hong Kong by South China Printing Co. (1988) Ltd.

Book Design by Tania Garcia
Book Production by Our House

The text is set in 16 point Bembo
The illustrations are rendered in watercolor
10 9 8 7 6 5 4 3 2 1
First Edition

Library of Congress Cataloging-in-Publication Data
Haggerty, Mary Elizabeth
A Crack In The Wall/ written by Mary Elizabeth Haggerty;
illustrated by Rubén De Anda
p. cm.
Summary: While his mother tries to find another job,
Carlos creates something special out of a crack in
the wall of their small apartment.
ISBN 1-880000-03-2
[1. Unemployment—Fiction. 2. Mothers and sons—Fiction.]
I. De Anda, Rubén, ill. II. Title
PZ7.H12455Cr 1993
[E]—dc20 92-59952 CIP AC

To my children and grandchildren,
present and future —M.E.H.

To my wife Maria, my son Israel,
and my mother Rosa —R.D.

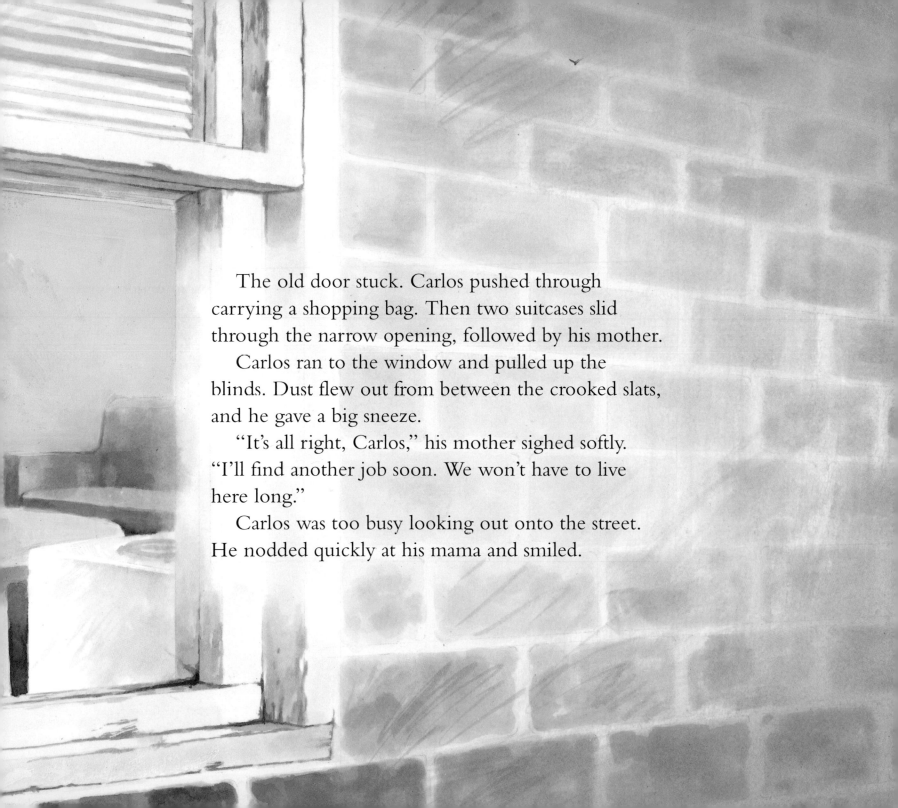

The old door stuck. Carlos pushed through carrying a shopping bag. Then two suitcases slid through the narrow opening, followed by his mother.

Carlos ran to the window and pulled up the blinds. Dust flew out from between the crooked slats, and he gave a big sneeze.

"It's all right, Carlos," his mother sighed softly. "I'll find another job soon. We won't have to live here long."

Carlos was too busy looking out onto the street. He nodded quickly at his mama and smiled.

Afternoon shadows had squeezed out all the daylight. Exhausted, Carlos and his mother decided to sleep early. He lay on the mattress listening to his mother's light snoring. He felt warm and safe when Mama snored. Mama wasn't worrying when she snored, and if Mama didn't worry, neither did he.

Carlos had rolled over on his side and started to close his eyes when the headlights of a passing car lit the wall. He sat up and screamed, "Mama, Mama!"

"What is it?" said Mama, grabbing Carlos and holding him close. "What is it?"

"There's something long and black crawling on the wall," said Carlos, terrified. Just then another car passed by, lighting up the wall again.

"Oh, Carlos, it's only a crack in the wall," said Mama with relief. "You mustn't let it scare you. Just close your eyes and think about something happy. Think about school. You like school."

But Mama's advice didn't work. Instead, Carlos pulled the quilt over his head and squeezed his eyes closed, hoping the crack would go away.

In the morning Mama made sure Carlos was all clean and shiny.

"Here is the key," she said, slipping a string over his head. "Come straight home. Remember, you'll have to push hard on the door, then lock it and don't open it for anyone but me. Do you understand?"

"Yes, Mama."

She gave him a kiss. "Just you wait. I'll get a new job and we'll move back to a better place soon...real soon."

After school Carlos did just as Mama told him. He sat on the floor and played marbles. But his eyes kept going to the crack in the wall. It wasn't as scary in the daytime. It almost looked like a tree branch. His mother loved trees. She would take him to the park just to see the trees.

That night when the cars drove by, Carlos imagined that the crack was a tree, all green and full of leaves like the ones in the park.

When Carlos came home the next afternoon, he
locked the door behind him, reached into his
pocket, and pulled out a fat green crayon. He
pulled the table over to the wall and began to color.

When he finished he pulled the table back and
admired his tree. Then he played marbles until
Mama came home.

But Mama was too tired to notice what Carlos had done. Carlos worried about Mama, and he worried about what Mama was worrying about.

"Did you get a job today, Mama?"

"Not yet, Carlos. Not yet."

That night there weren't many cars going by, and Carlos couldn't see his tree. If he couldn't see the tree in the dark, then neither could Mama, and she was hardly ever home in the daylight.

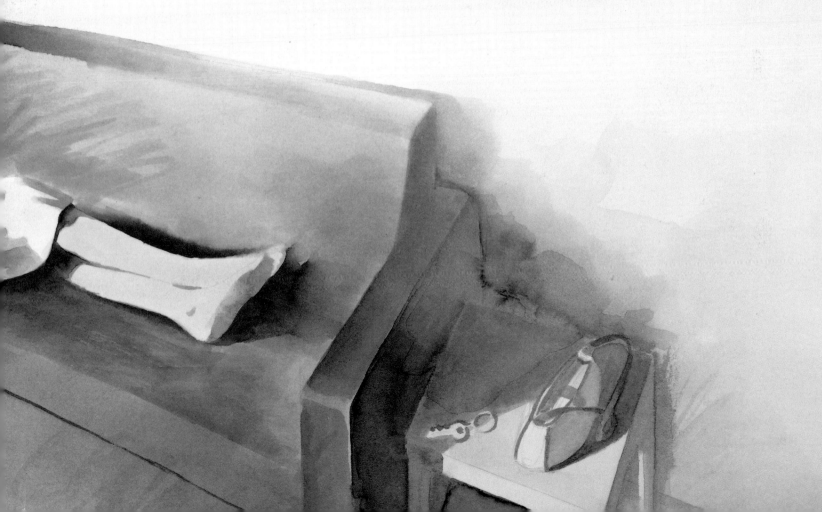

"Here's your milk money, Carlos. Have a nice day at school," said Mama the next morning.

"I will. We're making Christmas stars today."

"Christmas stars? Is it Christmastime already?" Mama asked with a worried frown on her face.

The door stuck more than usual that afternoon, and Carlos gave it a mighty kick. He pulled a pack of gum out of his pocket and spread the sticks on the table. Then he slid the paper wrapper off each one and undid the foil and very carefully smoothed it out.

He popped a stick of gum into his mouth and chewed with great concentration. When all the flavor was gone, he put the chewed piece of gum on the paper wrapper and popped in another stick of gum, chewing again, and again, and again, until all the gum had been chewed.

Then Carlos took the foil and folded each piece
into a star just as they had done in school that day.
He turned the stars over and put a wad of gum
right in the center of each star. Next he pulled the
table over to the wall where his tree grew and,
standing on tiptoe, he stuck each star into its special
place in the heavens.

When Carlos climbed down to admire his work,
he was disappointed. His Christmas stars looked
like gum wrappers. He climbed back up to take
them down but the gum stretched between the star
and the wall in long, sticky strands. He stuck the
star back on the wall.

He had wanted it to be pretty for Mama. Now
what was she going to say?

But Mama didn't notice the stars. She just said, "How was school today, Carlos?"

"It was fun. We made Christmas stars."

"That's nice," Mama said with a yawn. Then she lay down on the mattress and was soon fast asleep.

Carlos's heart was heavy. He had wanted to make the ugly room pretty for his mother, but he had only messed it up. And Mama hadn't noticed anyway.

He looked at the ugly crack in the wall. That's all it is, he thought. Just an ugly old crack in the wall. He laid down next to Mama and fell asleep.

"Carlos, wake up," Mama whispered, shaking him gently. "Wake up."

He stirred unwillingly and shut his eyes tighter.

"Carlos, wake up!" said Mama again. "Look at the wall. We have stars on our wall!" There was wonder in her voice.

Still sleepy, Carlos sat up and asked, "Do you like them, Mama? I made them for you. They're Christmas stars."

"Oh, Carlos, they are just beautiful." She got out of bed and walked toward the tree. Then she turned to Carlos and smiled. "Let's celebrate!" she said.

Carlos took her hand, and the two of them twirled and whirled under the sparkling stars.

Carlos and his mother danced until their feet
grew heavy. Then they snuggled back under the
quilt and watched the stars shine softly in the night.
When Carlos heard Mama snoring lightly, he
drifted off to sleep.